POSTCARDS FROM ALL OVER

Written by Cecilia Minden and Joanne Meier • Illustrated by Bob Ostrom
Created by Herbie J. Thorpe

ABOUT THE AUTHORS

Cecilia Minden, PhD, is the former director of the Language and Literacy Program at the Harvard Graduate School of Education. She is now a reading consultant for school and library publications. She earned her PhD in reading education from the University of Virginia. Cecilia and her husband, Dave Cupp, live outside Chapel Hill, North Carolina. They enjoy sharing their love of reading with their grandchildren, Chelsea and Qadir.

Joanne Meier, PhD, has worked as an elementary school teacher, university professor, and researcher. She earned her BA in early childhood education from the University of South Carolina, and her MEd and PhD in education from the University of Virginia. She currently works as a literacy consultant for schools and private organizations. Joanne lives in Virginia with her husband Eric, daughters Kella and Erin, two cats, and a gerbil.

ABOUT THE ILLUSTRATOR

Bob Ostrom has been illustrating children's books for nearly twenty years. A graduate of the New England School of Art & Design at Suffolk University, Bob has worked for such companies as Disney, Nickelodeon, and Cartoon Network. He lives in North Carolina with his wife Melissa and three children, Will, Charlie, and Mae.

ABOUT THE SERIES CREATOR

Herbie J. Thorpe had long envisioned a beginning-readers' series about a fun, energetic bear with a big imagination. Herbie is a book lover and an avid supporter of libraries and the role they play in fostering the love of reading. He consults with librarians and matches them with the perfect books for their students and patrons. He lives in Louisiana with his wife Misty and their daughter Carson.

Published in the United States of America by The Child's World®
1980 Lookout Drive • Mankato, MN 56003-1705
800-599-READ • www.childsworld.com

Acknowledgments
The Child's World®: Mary Berendes, Publishing Director
The Design Lab: Kathleen Petelinsek, Design;
Kari Tobin, Page Production
Artistic Assistant: Richard Carbajal

Library of Congress Cataloging-in-Publication Data
Minden, Cecilia.
  Postcards from all over / by Cecilia Minden and Joanne Meier ;
illustrated by Bob Ostrom.
    p. cm. — (Herbster readers)
  ISBN 978-1-60253-223-6 (library bound : alk. paper)
  [1. Postal service—Fiction. 2. Postcards—Fiction. 3. Bears—Fiction.] I. Meier, Joanne D. II. Ostrom, Bob, ill. III. Title. IV. Series.

PZ7.M6539Pos 2009
[E]—dc22   2009003998

Herbie Bear had a new class project.

"We're asking friends and family members to send postcards to our school," he told Dad.

"We're trying to get postcards from all fifty states."

"What a good project," said Dad.
"We'd better get started."

Herbie thought of six people.
"How do I tell them about the
project?" he asked.

"Write each person a letter," said Dad.
"Tell them about the project."

"Be sure to tell them where to send the postcard, too."

Herbie worked on his letter. It took a couple of tries. He carefully made six copies.

Herbie put the letters in envelopes. He wrote his own address in the left corner. He wrote the person's address in the middle.

"Where can I mail these?" asked Herbie.

"Let's take a walk to the post office," said Dad.

As they walked, Herbie asked questions. "What happens at the post office? How do my letters get where I want them to go?"

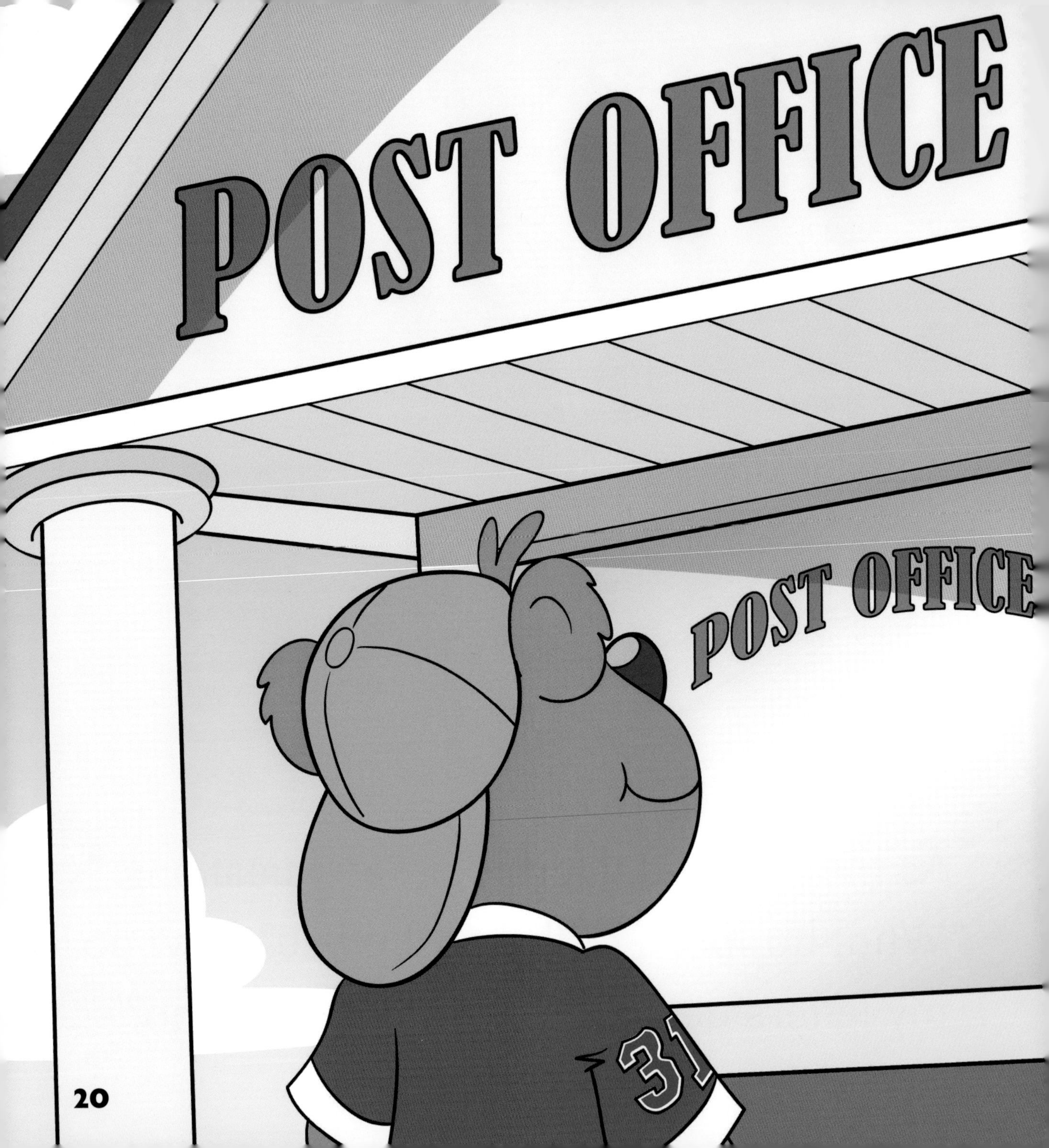
POST OFFICE
POST OFFICE
31

"Good questions, Herbie," said Dad.
"Here we are. Let's see what we can find out."

"First, we need to buy stamps," said Dad.

"That's how we pay the post office for delivering our mail. The mail carrier can't deliver mail without a stamp."

"Next," said Dad, "we put the letters in the mail slot."

"The mail goes down a chute and into a big bin. Workers sort the mail into bags."

"The bags are sent to post offices all over the country," said Dad. "Some go on trucks, but most go on big airplanes."

"When the bags reach other post offices, they are sorted again," said Dad. "Mail carriers pick them up. Then they deliver the letters to people."

"I can't wait for my letters to get delivered," said Herbie.

Two weeks later, Herbie got six postcards in the mail. He proudly put them on the classroom map.

The class received many great postcards.

Herbie looked at the map and smiled.